DATE DUE

THEA'S TREE

Judith Clay

In the city where Thea lived, there were only houses, houses, and more houses.

They were cold and high and without joy.

Mama told Thea about all the trees of her childhood… trees to climb, trees to hide in, trees to sit under and dream.

Papa told Thea about all the fun they had in summertime, picking mangoes and guavas and neem leaves to eat.

Thea really wished she had a tree.

One day, late in October, a beautiful leaf came floating gently and quietly past Thea's window. Her ears were filled with the sound of rustling leaves.

'Where there's a leaf, there has to be a tree,' Thea thought. 'I have to find it!'

Thea saw her friends playing on the street and stopped. She pointed to the leaf that was dancing in the wind.

'Do you want to help me find its tree?' Thea asked. 'We'll then have our very own climbing tree to play in.'

But her friends didn't seem to understand the importance of finding the tree. Perhaps they didn't even know what a tree was.

Thea followed the leaf, her arm outstretched, determined.

Every time she came close to it, a strange melody of rustling leaves filled the air.

Round and round, the leaf led her on a chase. Suddenly, it rose up in the air and Thea found herself rising with it.

Valiantly, she reached out once more – and finally managed to grab the leaf.

As Thea clutched on to the leaf, the rustling melody suddenly washed over her and Thea could not help drifting off to sleep.

The leaf lifted her up, high above the concrete
city, and soared with her towards the moon
and the stars.

She found herself near a beautiful tree with white leaves and a wise, old face. The tree saw right into Thea's heart and found her deepest desire.

'Why do you want a tree, my dear?' the tree asked gently. 'Do you want to build a hut or a boat or a fire with it? Do you want to make it into newspapers and books?'

Thea shook her head. Shyly, she said, 'I want a tree for climbing and playing and to sit and dream under.'

'Then go plant this seed,' said the wise, white tree, 'And give it water and love and conversation.'

When Thea awoke, she was outside her house, clutching the seed.

Her heart bursting with her dream, she planted the seed in a small patch of ground. She watered it everyday and loved it everyday and talked to it everyday.

And one day, a small plant emerged.

As Thea grew older, so did the tree. Thea's children played and dreamed under it, and Thea's grandchildren.

And if you come to Thea's town today, you will find it there still.